THEYTUS BOOKS

Zoe and the Fawn

Catherine Jameson
with illustrations by Julie Flett

Dedicated to Zoe

Zoe and her dad go outside to give the horses (*snkɬcaʔ sqaẋaʔ*) food and water. Dad brings his camera to take pictures of the new foal (*sqayksqaẋaʔ*).

Outside the yard Zoe and her dad see something
moving under a tree.
"What can that be?" Zoe asks.
"Let us go look," says Dad.

Zoe and her dad see a little spotted fawn
(*sk'ʷek'ʷƛ'il't*) curled up under an aspen tree.
Zoe and her dad go to take a closer look.
"But not too close," says Dad.

Zoe and the fawn *(sk'ᵂek'ᵂƛ'il't)* look at each other.
Zoe smiles and the fawn's ears perk up.
Dad takes a picture.

"Where is the fawn's *(sk'ʷek'ʷƛ'il't)* mother?"
Zoe asks her dad.
Zoe and her dad look all around the grove.
"Let us go look for her," says Dad.

They walk over a small hill covered with flowers and see a beautiful red flicker (*kʷəlkʷ əlˤakn*) land in a tree.

"Is that bird the fawn's mother?" Zoe asks.
"No, it is not," says Dad.
"Where can she be?" Zoe wonders.

They look in the tall green grass and find a small brown rabbit (*k'ʷək'ʷyumaʔ spəplinaʔ*) sleeping soundly.

"Is that rabbit the fawn's mother (*iʔ tum'təms*)?"
Zoe asks.
"No, it is not," says Dad.
"Where can she be?" Zoe wonders.

Zoe and her dad walk further past the green grass and down to the creek.
They see a rainbow trout $(x^wumina\mathtt{?})$ jumping in the water.

"Is that fish the fawn's mother?" Zoe asks.
"No, it is not," says Dad.
"Where can she be?" Zoe wonders.

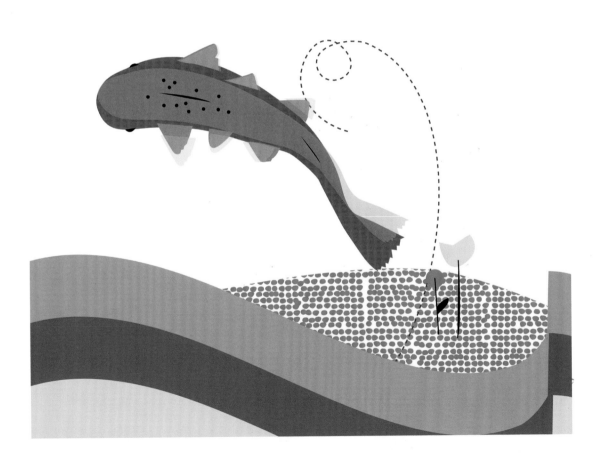

Beyond the creek, Zoe and her dad look all around but do not see the fawn's mother.

So they turn around and walk back
toward the creek.

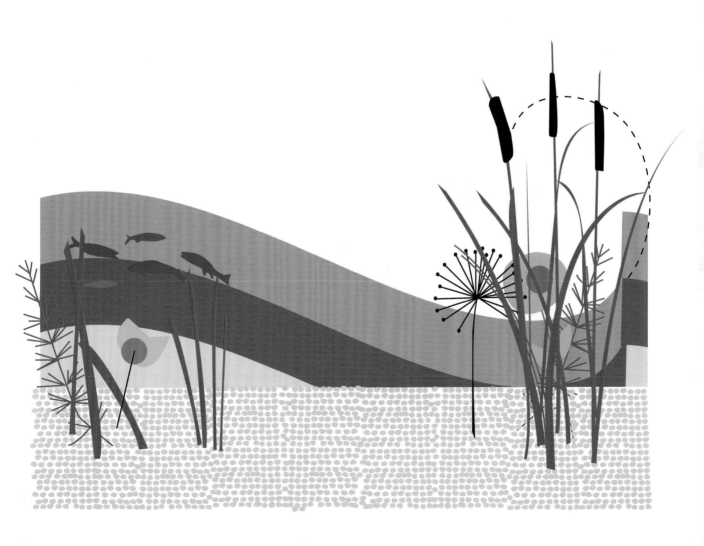

They see the rainbow trout ($x^w umina$?) jump and swim deep.
Zoe says, "That is not the fawn's mother."

They walk through the tall green grass and see the little brown rabbit (*k'ʷək'ʷyumaʔ spəplinaʔ*) hop away.

Zoe says, "That is not the fawn's mother."

They walk over a small hill covered with flowers and see the beautiful red flicker (*kʷəlkʷ əlʕakn*) fly away.
Zoe says, "That is not the fawn's mother."

Zoe and her dad look all around.
"Where can she be?" sighs Zoe.
They walk down the other side of the small hill
through the wild flowers.

"Look! The fawn (*sk'ʷek'ʷƛ'il't*) and her mother!" says Zoe. They are curled up under the aspen tree. Zoe smiles and the fawn's ears perk up. Dad takes another picture.

"Now we will go finish our chores," says dad, and the horses *(snkɫcaʔ sqax̌aʔ)* whinny with delight.

Zoe and the Fawn
2nd Printing
© 2006 Catherine Jameson
Illustrations © 2006 Julie Flett

Library and Archives Canada Cataloguing in Publication

Jameson, Catherine
Zoe and the fawn / by Catherine Jameson ;illustrated by Julie Flett.

For ages 1-5.
ISBN 1-894778-43-X

I.Flett, Julie II.Title.

PS8619.A6635Z45 2006   jC813'.6   C2006-904460-0

Printed in Canada

THEYTUS BOOKS

www.theytus.com

In Canada: Theytus Books, Green Mountain Rd., Lot 45, RR#2, Site 50, Comp. 8
Penticton, BC, V2A 6J7, Tel: 250-493-7181

In the USA: Theytus Books, P.O. Box 2890, Oroville, Washington, 98844

Patrimoine   Canadian
canadien   Heritage

Canada Council   Conseil des Arts
for the Arts   du Canada

BRITISH COLUMBIA
ARTS COUNCIL
Supported by the Province of British Columbia

Theytus Books acknowledges the support of the following:
We acknowledge the financial support of the Government of Canada through the
Canada Book Fund for our publishing activities. We acknowledge the support of
the Canada Council for the Arts which last year invested $20.1 million in writing
and publishing throughout Canada. Nous remercions de son soutien le Conseil des
Arts du Canada, qui a investi 20,1 millions de dollars l'an dernier dans les lettres
et l'édition à travers le Canada. We acknowledge the support of the Province of
British Columbia through the British Columbia Arts Council.